Our Principal Promised to Kiss a Pig

To Colleen,
Have fun
with
Hamlet!

Kalli
Dakos
4-2-18

Kalli Dakos and **Alicia DesMarteau**

Pictures by **Carl DiRocco**

Albert Whitman & Company
Chicago, Illinois

For the memory of my Aunt Irene,
whose love of great literature
inspired my childhood,
and for the entire Sperdakos Family—KD

To God for saving me,
and to Grandma for making me Greek noodles—AD

For Gina, James, David, and Mark—CD

Library of Congress Cataloging-in-Publication Data

Dakos, Kalli.
Our principal promised to kiss a pig / by Kalli Dakos and Alicia DesMarteau;
illustrated by Carl DiRocco.
p. cm.
Summary: When the school principal promises to kiss a pig if the students read 10,000 books,
a girl volunteers Hamlet, her unwilling, Shakespeare-quoting pet pig.
[1. Books and reading—Fiction. 2. Pigs—Fiction. 3. School principals—Fiction. 4. Schools—Fiction.
5. Shakespeare, William, 1564–1616—Fiction.]
I. DesMarteau, Alicia. II. DiRocco, Carl, ill. III. Title.
PZ7.D15223Ou 2004
[Fic]–dc22
2003026210

Printed in China
10 9 8 7 6 5 4 3 2 1 LP 20 19 18 17 16

Design by Carol Gildar

For more information about Albert Whitman & Company,
visit our web site at www.albertwhitman.com.

My pet pig, Hamlet, knows about broken hearts,
and it's all my fault.

It started in September when the principal of my school said she would kiss a pig if the students read lots of books. Ms. Juliet loves to do crazy things to get us to read. Last year she went up in a hot-air balloon, even though she is terrified of heights, and her screams were so loud they scared the toupee off the gym teacher's head.

Another year she sat on the roof of the school for an entire day and read books. When it started to rain, she put on scuba-diving goggles and a snorkel and kept right on reading.

This year she has promised to kiss a pig if we read 10,000 books.

It just so happened that I have a pig! My aunt won a pet pig at the state fair last year and gave him to me when she moved into an apartment that doesn't allow pets. She teaches high school students about a man called William Shakespeare. He was a writer hundreds of years ago. People spoke a funny kind of English back then and had weird names like Romeo, Touchstone, and Hamlet. My aunt thought it would be funny to name her pig Hamlet.

Without even thinking, I told Ms. Juliet all about my pig and volunteered him for the kiss. Poor Hamlet! When I told him, he looked as if I was going to make him eat a ham sandwich.

I should never have opened my big mouth and said Ms. Juliet could kiss him in front of the entire school. I wouldn't want someone to kiss me in front of hundreds of people. Why would a pig feel any different?

All the kids at school started reading. By the end of November, we had read 1,428 books. Ms. Juliet made us figure out how many more we had to read.

$$10,000 - 1,428 = 8,572 \text{ books}$$

At least Hamlet didn't have to kiss the principal...yet. But I knew he was worried when I found him at the stove stirring pizza sauce, mud, and prune juice in a huge pot. I think he was trying to make a magic potion to stop the kiss!

By the end of April, we had read 4,702 books. We still had 5,298 left. The school year was nearly over, and we hadn't even read half the books to win the contest!

In May, two things happened. An author came to visit our school, and we had the best book fair in the world.

One girl in my class bought 26 books with her dog-walking money and read every single one of them. A lot of kids started reading the author's books, and before long we had read 8,987 books.

Hamlet was miserable.

I guess his potion didn't work.

Out, out, brief candle
With so small a light!
My hopes are fading
On this dark night.

The third week in May, Hamlet's fate was sealed. The kids had read 10,682 books and were still reading.

A day in June was picked for the kiss. The newspaper planned to send a reporter and a photographer. The gym was decorated with over 10,000 hearts and lips—one for every book we'd read. The night before the big kiss, Hamlet stayed in my room. Neither of us could sleep.

The next morning, I put Hamlet in the baby's car seat, and my mother drove us to school. I felt sick inside and didn't even want to imagine how Hamlet felt.

But when we arrived at school, I saw a stubborn look on Hamlet's face.

All the world's a stage,
And one pig in his time
Plays many parts.

I must be a soldier
In this kissing war—
The battle starts!

The kids cheered when I walked into the gym with Hamlet. We walked past 10,983 hearts and lips to a big table. I put Hamlet on the table and stayed beside him for support. What was going to happen next?

Ms. Juliet walked into the gym, and the students cheered again. When Hamlet saw her, he gasped and nearly fell off the table. Then his eyes lit up as if the sun, the moon, and the stars had all come out at once. I could tell he had changed his mind about kissing Ms. Juliet!

Ms. Juliet announced, "Congratulations, students. You have won the contest again this year. Now I will honor my promise and kiss this...pig." She leaned over to kiss Hamlet on the snout. Hamlet leaned forward too, ready and waiting for the kiss...but it never came.

Then in the silence of the gym, Ms. Juliet took a step away from Hamlet and said in a voice that was just above a whisper, "I was able to go up in that hot-air balloon, even though I am afraid of heights. I was able to sit on the roof of the school for an entire day, even in the rain. But the very thought of kissing a pig brings dirt, mud, and slop to my mind, and I can't do it. I just can't!"

The kids started yelling, "You have to kiss the pig. You promised! You promised!"

Ms. Juliet looked around the room at the hearts and lips, the photographer, the reporter, the teachers, and the students. Then she looked at Hamlet, who was almost in tears.

Ms. Juliet moved closer to the table where Hamlet was waiting, leaned over, and looked into his eyes. As if in a dream, Hamlet gazed back at her.

Then Ms. Juliet puckered her lips and kissed Hamlet on the snout—not once, not twice, but three times! Hamlet looked as though he was going to faint.

All the kids clapped and cheered. Hamlet was still in a daze when I picked him up. His eyes were round and dopey and glued to Ms. Juliet.

Hamlet wasn't the same after the big kiss. He couldn't sleep, he hardly ate, and he moped around the house.

Ms. Juliet, my star above,
I no sooner looked than loved.

I'll be sad today and tomorrow,
For parting is such sweet sorrow.

I was worried about him, so I was relieved when my aunt told me she'd won another pig at the state fair this year—a girl pig! My aunt named her Kate and brought her over to keep Hamlet company. I think Hamlet's broken heart is healing fast.

There's one thing our story proves—
the course of true love can run smooth!